big&SMALL

Original Korean text by Seong-eun Gahng
Illustrations by Gwang-pil Jeong
Korean edition © Yeowon Media Co., Ltd.

This English edition published by Big & Small in 2015
by arrangement with Yeowon Media Co., Ltd.
English text edited by Joy Cowley
English edition © Big & Small 2015

ISBN: 978-1-921790-84-3

Printed in Korea

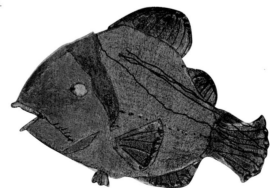

The Golden Fish

A story by Alexander Pushkin
retold by Joy Cowley
Illustrated by Gwang-pil Jeong

An old man and an old woman
lived in a little old hut by the sea.
The old woman spun yarn
with her spinning wheel
while the old man went fishing
in his little boat.

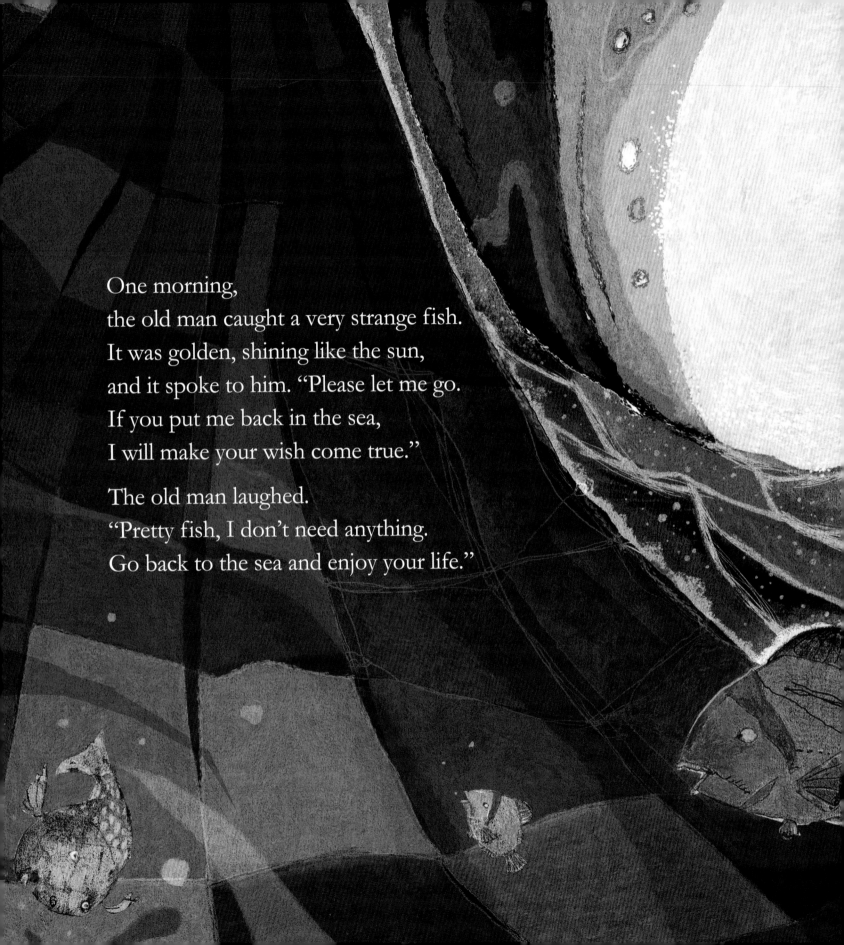

One morning,
the old man caught a very strange fish.
It was golden, shining like the sun,
and it spoke to him. "Please let me go.
If you put me back in the sea,
I will make your wish come true."

The old man laughed.
"Pretty fish, I don't need anything.
Go back to the sea and enjoy your life."

6

When the old woman heard the story
of the golden fish, she was angry.
She yelled at her husband,
"Why didn't you make a wish?
We are poor! Our house is falling apart!
Look at my broken basket!"

The old man got in his boat
and went out on the sea again.
"Golden fish! Golden fish!" he called.

At once, the fish came up beside the boat.
"What do you want?" it asked.

"My wife needs a new basket,"
said the old man.

The golden fish splashed its tail.
"She will have a new basket.
Your wish will come true."

11

The old man went home.
Yes, there it was! A new basket!

But the old woman was still angry.
She yelled at her husband, "You fool!
You wished for a silly basket!
Go back to that golden fish
and ask for a new house!"

Back to the sea the old man went.
"Golden fish! Golden fish!" he called.

The fish came up. "What do you want?"

The old man wrung his hands. "Please!
My wife says she wants a new house."

The fish flipped its tail. "Go back.
Your wish will come true."

The old hut had been replaced
by a solid, brand-new house.
But his wife was still not satisfied.

"You old fool!" she screamed.
"You wished for a small house!
Go out to the golden fish right now.
I want to be a lady in a big mansion."

The old man went out to sea again.
The waves lapped against his boat,
as he called for the golden fish.

"What is it this time?" asked the fish.

"I am sorry, golden fish. It's my wife.
She is unhappy with a small house.
She wants to live in a big mansion."

"Don't worry," said the golden fish.
"Your wish will come true."

When the old man went home,
his mouth opened in amazement.
He saw a big mansion in a fine garden,
and his wife dressed like a noble lady.
"I like your new clothes," he said.

His wife would not look at him.
"You are an old fisherman," she said.
"You can go and live in the stable."

A few days passed,
and the old woman called the old man.
"Go and tell that golden fish
that I want to be queen of all the land."

"My dear," said the old man,
"please, don't be greedy."

The old woman screamed at him,
"Do as I say! I want to be queen!"

The sky and sea were dark
and great waves hit the boat.
The old man shouted over the wind,
"Golden fish, I am afraid!
My wife wants to be queen
of all the land."

It was a long time
before the fish answered.
"All right, old man," it said
in a voice like thunder.
"Your wish will come true."

Where the fine mansion had been,
there stood a huge shining palace.
But the old woman was still unhappy.
She screamed at her poor husband,
"I am only queen of the land!
I have to be queen of the sea, as well.
Go back in your boat, old fool!
Say that I want to be queen of the sea
and I want that golden fish
to be my servant!"

The old man went out on the sea
where a wild storm was raging.
He cried to the golden fish,
"I'm sorry, but my wife is still unhappy.
She wants to be queen of the sea
as well as queen of the land,
and she wants you to be her servant."

This time, the fish did not say anything.
It disappeared under the wild waves.

When the golden fish did not return,
the old man went back to the shore.

The shining palace had gone.
There was only the little old hut
and at the door stood the old woman,
holding the broken basket in her hand.